Ursula by the Sea

Sheila Lavelle

Illustrated by
Thelma Lambert

Hamish Hamilton
London

JF

HAMISH HAMILTON CHILDREN'S BOOKS

Published by the Penguin Group
27 Wrights Lane, London W8 5TZ, England
Viking Penguin Inc, 40 West 23rd Street, New York, New York 10010, U.S.A.
Penguin Books Australia Ltd, Ringwood, Victoria, Australia
Penguin Books Canada Ltd, 2801 John Street, Markham, Ontario, Canada L3R 1B4
Penguin Books (N.Z.) Ltd, 182-190 Wairau Road, Auckland 10, New Zealand

Penguin Books Ltd, Registered Offices: Harmondsworth, Middlesex, England

7328
/

First published in Great Britain 1986 by
Hamish Hamilton Children's Books

Text copyright © 1986 by Sheila Lavelle
Illustrations copyright © 1986 by Thelma Lambert

Reprinted 1988

British Library Cataloguing in Publication Data
Lavelle, Sheila
Ursula by the sea.—(Cartwheels)
I. Title   II. Lambert, Thelma   III. Series
823'.914[J]   PZ7

ISBN 0-241-11914-6

Typeset by Katerprint Typesetting Services, Oxford
Printed in Great Britain by
Cambus Litho Ltd
East Kilbride, Scotland

Ursula had sixteen teddy bears in her bed
and she loved every one. But the one she
loved most was Fredbear.

Fredbear had lost an eye and hadn't
much fur left, but still Ursula loved him
best of all.

She knitted him a red jumper to keep
his bald tummy warm, and she sang him
to sleep every night.

Ursula lived with her Aunt Prudence. One sunny morning she came downstairs and found her aunt in the kitchen, wearing a new yellow sun-dress.

Aunt Prudence was packing a picnic basket with ham sandwiches, sausage rolls and chocolate cake.

"Put on your shorts and sandals,
Ursula," said Aunt Prudence. "We're
going to the seaside."

"Hooray!" shouted Ursula, dancing round the table. "Have you packed me a currant bun?"

"Of course," smiled Aunt Prudence. "With your favourite filling of porridge oats and honey."

Ursula ran to fetch her bucket and spade.

Aunt Prudence knew that Ursula loved
bears. But she didn't know that Ursula
had a very special secret.

Ursula's secret was a magic spell. A
spell that could turn her from an ordinary
girl into a *real, live bear*.

And all she needed was a currant bun,
filled with a mixture of porridge oats and
honey.

Aunt Prudence put the picnic basket in the car.

Fredbear sat on Ursula's knee and gazed out of the window. He looked very smart in his new red jumper.

The sun was shining and Ursula sang all the way to Sandy Bay.

Aunt Prudence parked the car and
Ursula helped to carry everything down
to a quiet part of the beach.

"This looks like a nice place," said
Aunt Prudence. She set up her deckchair
near some rocks.

Ursula looked at the waves sparkling in the sunshine. She pulled off her socks and sandals.

"I'm going for a paddle," she said.

"Be careful," warned Aunt Prudence. "I think the tide's coming in."

13

Ursula tucked Fredbear under her arm, picked up her bucket and spade, and ran over the warm sand towards the sea.

She splashed in and out of the water and jumped over the waves.

After a while Ursula began to build a sandcastle.

She made walls and towers and bridges, and she even dug a moat and filled it with water.

It was the best sandcastle Ursula had ever made.

When it was finished Ursula sat
Fredbear on the top. She made a flag
from a lollipop stick and a paper hanky,
and gave it to Fredbear to hold.

"Guard the castle, Fredbear," she said.
"I'm going to buy an ice-cream."

The café was a long way across the
beach and Ursula had to wait ages in the
queue.

On her way back with the ice-cream she heard children shouting and laughing. It was a Punch and Judy Show, and Ursula just had to stop and watch.

Ursula enjoyed herself so much that she forgot all about Fredbear waiting by the castle.

Then all at once she remembered.

She raced across the sand to where she had left him.

Ursula stopped and stared and her eyes grew rounder and rounder.

There was no sandcastle, and no
bucket and spade, and no Fredbear.

The tide had come in and washed them
all away.

Ursula gazed out to sea. She saw a few
seagulls and a sailing boat with a white
sail.

Then she noticed a small red shape bobbing up and down in the water.

It was Fredbear.

Teddy bears can't swim, and Ursula had to do something quickly. But what? She knew she couldn't swim that far either, and it would be stupid to try.

And then all at once Ursula had an idea.

"Teddy bears can't swim," she said to herself. "But *real* bears can!"

She dashed up the beach towards Aunt Prudence.

Aunt Prudence was fast asleep in the deckchair, her knitting in her lap.

Ursula quickly opened the picnic basket and took out the currant bun, with the special magic mixture.

She hid among the rocks and began to gobble the bun as fast as she could.

"I'M A BEAR, I'M A BEAR, I'M A BEAR," she mumbled, dropping crumbs all over her best shorts.

A seagull flying by almost dropped his fish in surprise. For Ursula had disappeared, and in her place a small brown bear was dancing about in the sand.

Ursula had turned into Ursula Bear.

Ursula Bear scampered back down the beach and splashed into the sea.

She swam as hard as she could, to where Fredbear was now only a tiny red dot in the distance.

The waves got up her nose and in her
ears, but Ursula managed to reach
Fredbear at last.

She was only just in time, for the water
had soaked through his fur and he was
beginning to sink.

Ursula grabbed him and swam towards the shore.

She ran along the beach with Fredbear safe in her arms.

Now she had to turn back into a girl again, and this time she needed beefburger and chips to make the magic work.

There was only one place to get beefburger and chips, and that was the café.

Ursula peeped in at the back door of the café. There was nobody about, and she wondered if she dared go in.

Suddenly she darted behind some
dustbins as a boy came out with some
scraps for the seagulls.

Beefburger and chips! Just what Ursula
needed!

The boy went back inside and Ursula
quickly snatched some of the food. She
had to fight the seagulls over it, and they
screamed in fury.

Then Ursula crouched behind the bins, to eat her few scraps. She grunted the magic words backwards as she chewed.

"RAEB A M'I, RAEB A M'I, RAEB A M'I," she growled.

A minute later there was Ursula, in her blue shorts and striped T-shirt, and quite herself again.

She hurried back to her aunt.

Ursula took off Fredbear's wet jumper and sat him on a rock in the sunshine to dry.

Aunt Prudence opened her eyes.

"What shall we do now, Ursula?" she said.

Ursula remembered the basket of ham sandwiches and sausage rolls and chocolate cake.

"Let's have lunch," she said. "I'm starving!" And she began to spread the picnic out on the sand.